This book belongs to...

....

....

I dedicate this book to my mum Jane, she really is a beautiful soul and without her – life wouldn't be quite as special.

Special mentions and thanks

I would firstly like to thank my amazing illustrator – Jo Blake for all of her hard work, impeccable designs and her commitment to ensure my books are as beautifully crafted as possible.
Not only is she my illustrator, but she is one of my favourite people to connect with, her value is priceless and now she is a great friend for life.

I need to also mention the amazing authors group I am part of, they always provide support, kindness and great energy.
So I thank you all for being you! (You know who you are.)

look out for Dexxy hiding in the book! ♡

ISBN: 9798717738613

Is She The Most Embarrassing Mum In Town?

Written by
Gemma Bond

Illustrated by
Jo Blake

Willow doesn't think her mum
is funny at all,
she gets embarrassed when
her mum acts the fool,

when she makes silly
jokes and acts so daft –

Willow doesn't think her mum is a blast!

"Let's go little chick, we're off to the park. We must hurry up
before it's too dark."
"Okay, mummy, I can't wait to play."
Willow exclaims, "It's a beautiful day!"

They both jump excitedly out of the car, the park is in sight, it isn't far.
Willow spins round to speak to her mum and notices **Mum's skirts up showing her bum!**

"Oh no, Not again, you're embarrassing me."
People are staring, mum's face full of glee.
"Oh Willow what's wrong, what have I done now?"
"Your skirt is stuck up — this is funny, how?"

Off they go – the zip wire is their first choice,
Willow jumps on, screams at the top of her voice.
"Wey hey mum, this is so great!!"
Mums turn next, she cannot wait.

Cake
balloons
doll?

Mum grabs the cord and jumps on the seat,
pushing herself away with her feet.
All of a sudden she gives out a "roar",
Mum's pockets now empty all over the floor.

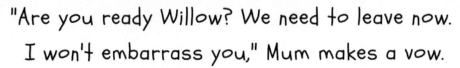

"Are you ready Willow? We need to leave now.
I won't embarrass you," Mum makes a vow.

While driving to school, Mum's singing away,
her favourite song starting to play.

RADIO BLAST

Cars drive past and the people smile,
"I haven't sung this loud in such a long while."
Willow shuts her eyes and covers her face.
Mum's jiggling around, all over the place.

"Oh not again, you're embarrassing me.
You're acting so crazy and just plain silly!"

Walking to school mum's feet start to slip,
for some reason she is losing her grip.

As she looks down, she gives a huge shriek,
it's the second time she's gone out in slippers this week.

"Oh no not again, you're embarrassing me".
Mum is just crazy, as crazy as can be.

I join Mum at work and watch her cut hair.
She pops a gown round and I start to stare.
A pair of her pants are stuck to the Velcro,
I just can't believe this – Oh no no no nooo!!

Mum grabs the pants, in her pocket they go.
Willow is hoping the client won't know.
Mum lets out a giggle and the client says "Okay?"
Mum replies "Yes fine, are you going on holiday?"

"Oh no, not again, you're
embarrassing me.
The silly things you do that
people all see."

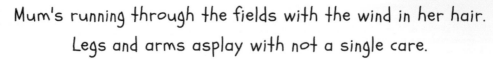

Mum's running through the fields with the wind in her hair.
Legs and arms asplay with not a single care.

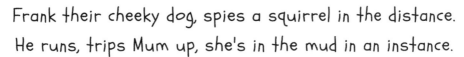

Frank their cheeky dog, spies a squirrel in the distance.
He runs, trips Mum up, she's in the mud in an instance.

All Willow can hear is Mum's chuckling sound.
Covered in mud, sprawled on the ground.
"Oh no, not again, you're embarrassing me.
Please stop these antics," Willow makes her plea.

As she crouches, Mum's bum makes the most terrible noise.
Everyone turns to look, even the toys!
She's let out the loudest and longest fart ever,
Willow wished they hadn't gone shopping together!

"Oh no, not again, you're embarrassing me."
The smell is so bad people start to flee.

"Yippee, Mum, it's finally my birthday!"
She spots her presents inside the doorway.
"Happy birthday to my gorgeous girl."
Willow's ecstatic – she moves with a twirl.

Off they go to the trampoline place, her friends arrive,
"This place is ace!"
Mum cannot wait, she starts to bounce.
Willow walks off with a moody flounce.
"Oh no, not again......!"

"Hey what's up – are you ok?"
Her friends all ask.
**"No – no way. My mum is so silly,
always embarrassing me."**
"But Willow, she's such fun, can't you see?"

Willow now knows that her Mum is so funny.
Making her friends giggle from deep in their tummy.
She always joins in and acts so daft,
"I love you Mum, you are a **blast**!!"

Gemma Bond, author of 'Dexxy the Determined Dragon', loves nothing more than to devise stories from her crazy imagination and Baye (her daughter) always plays a big part during the story creating process.

Living in Buckinghamshire (UK) as a single parent, author, hair artist, empath and reiki practitioner- Gemma loves helping others, being social and embarking on new challenges.

She loves nothing more than taking her daughter to exciting new places, from fairy festivals to surfing at the most beautiful beaches - adventuring and being in nature.

At their family home they have two beautiful pets - Alonso their 14 year old cat and Clover their crazy golden retriever.

Both Gemma and her daughter Baye have a "wicked" sense of humour, they both find fun in pretty much anything they do and there is NEVER a dull moment.

Gemma hope's to empower children to build resilience, inner strength and determination. Inspiring all children to see the magic in the world and breed general kindness - positivity amongst everyone.

Follow Gemma on Facebook @Gemmabondauthor Instagram @gem007gem
YouTube - Gemma Bond Author

Jo Blake illustrator/artist, lives in Devon with her family and much loved dog 'Blue'. When she isn't in her art studio, she is gaming, watching retro cartoons and being in the beautiful countryside.

Follow Jo on facebook and instagram @Joblakeart

ANOTHER BOOK
FROM THIS AUTHOR

Dexxy
The Determined Dragon!

Author
Gemma Bond

Illustrator
Jo Blake

Coming soon....

Is He The Most Embarrassing Dad In Town?
&
Dexxy The Determined Dragon 2

Is she the most

Embarrassing

mum in town?

Dexxy The Determined Dragon!

Printed in Great Britain
by Amazon